Thomas and the Treasure and Other Stories

Random House 🏠 New York

A Random House PICTUREBACK® Book

Photographs by Terry Palone and Terry Permane

Thomas the Tank Engine & Friends™

CREATED BY BRITT ALLCROFT

Based on The Railway Series by The Reverend W Awdry.

© 2008 Gullane (Thomas) LLC.

Thomas the Tank Engine & Friends and Thomas & Friends are trademarks of Gullane (Thomas) Limited.
Thomas the Tank Engine & Friends & Design is Reg. U.S. Pat. & Tm. Off.
www.randomhouse.com/kids/thomas   www.thomasandfriends.com

Library of Congress Control Number: 2007932551

ISBN 978-0-375-84287-0

Printed in the United States of America   10 9 8 7 6 5 4 3 2 1   First Edition

HiT entertainment

· THOMAS AND THE TREASURE ·

Brendam Docks is a very busy place. Engines bring freight cars . . . cranes unload cargo . . . and ships bring visitors.

One day, Thomas had to collect a very important visitor—the Admiral! Thomas was to take the Admiral to open the new Maritime Museum. It was a museum all about the sea.

Salty was excited. "The Admiral is always looking for the lost pirate treasure of Sodor!" he said.

"Pirates?" scoffed James.

"Treasure?" huffed Emily.

"Yes," said Salty. "But no one has ever found it!"

Salty told them there were three clues. "First, find the eagle of the mountains. Its beak will point to the clouds not in the sky. Then those clouds will lead to the skull and crossbones! And there you'll find the treasure, me hearties!"

"Eagle . . . clouds . . . skull and crossbones . . . ," tooted Thomas excitedly. "I'm sure I could solve those clues!"

Emily and James thought it was all nonsense! And that made Thomas cross.

Just then, the Admiral arrived!
Thomas puffed off to collect him.
The Admiral had to be at the
museum in time for the Grand
Opening. Thomas felt very proud to
be taking him.

"What if I arrived with the Admiral and a chest of pirate treasure!"
thought Thomas. "That would show James and Emily!"

So Thomas chuffed onto the track away from the museum and set off
into the mountains—to look for the first clue. . . .

"How could an eagle point the way?" wondered Thomas. "How could clouds not be in the sky?" And Thomas knew he had never seen a skull and crossbones anywhere. . . .

Later Emily puffed towards Thomas. "There's no such thing as treasure," she laughed.

But Thomas paid no attention. The eagle of the mountains had to be somewhere!

Then he saw something wonderful! A mountain that looked like an eagle!

Thomas was very excited. "I've found the first clue!" he hooted happily. "Now I'll find the next one!" The eagle's head would point the way!

Suddenly Thomas saw a track leading in the direction of the stone beak!

"Where are you going, Thomas?" *wheesh*ed James.

"To find the clouds that are not in the sky!" whistled Thomas.

"How silly!" snorted James. And he chuffed away.

But Thomas didn't mind. He knew the clouds were here somewhere! And then . . . he saw them! The clouds not in the sky . . . were reflections of clouds—in the lake!

"I've found the second clue!" *wheesh*ed Thomas excitedly. "One more and I'll find the treasure!" Thomas looked for a long time.

And he forgot all about the Admiral.

Then Harold arrived . . . with Sir Topham Hatt.

"The Admiral is late for the opening of the museum!" he boomed crossly. "You have been unreliable," added Sir Topham Hatt. "Harold will now take the Admiral to the museum."

Thomas felt very foolish. If only he hadn't spent so much time looking for the clues. . . .

"Fancy believing in a silly old story!" laughed Harold.

"Everyone thinks I'm silly," huffed Thomas, "but I still believe there's treasure!" Thomas puffed sadly along the track away from the lake.

Thomas had never been this way before. . . . So he didn't know where it would lead.

It led him into a tunnel!

At last, Thomas came to the end of the line. He was surprised!

There were all the other engines!

And there was the Admiral!

"I am very proud to declare the new Maritime Museum open!" he announced. Everyone cheered and whistled.

Then Thomas saw something even more exciting!

"That's it!" Thomas tooted. "The pirate's treasure's right here!"

"Don't be silly!" huffed Emily.

"Everyone knows it's just a silly old story!" snorted James.

But Thomas knew he was right. "I followed all the clues!" he puffed proudly.

"And you have found the skull and crossbones!" cried the Admiral.

Everyone was surprised!

"Someone get me a shovel!" The Admiral was so excited, he dug for the pirate treasure himself! He found a big wooden chest!

Inside was the pirate treasure!

"The pirate treasure will be the most important thing in the whole museum!" said the Admiral.

"Thomas," boomed Sir Topham Hatt, "you have made this the best opening ever!"

Thomas was very proud. He had been right to believe in Salty's story!

He had found the treasure!

• DUNCAN'S BLUFF •

It was wintertime on the Island of Sodor.

Duncan was busy puffing through the white mountains and the frosty forests. He was proud to be a narrow-gauge engine. Duncan was delivering coal to the villages. They were going to need extra coal from the main coaling plant!

So James and Thomas brought coal to the wharf.

Duncan chuffed in to talk to James.

"You were a long time getting here!" teased Duncan.

"You're lucky I came at all," *wheesh*ed James crossly. "I've got an important job to do later. I'm taking some children to a concert!"

"Oh! Is doing two jobs in one day too hard for you?" Duncan chuffed cheekily.

"Pah!" snorted James. "I can do more jobs in one day than you can! I'm Really Useful!"

This made Duncan cross.

"How about a wee contest?" chuffed Duncan. "I bet I can take more coal to the villages faster than you can deliver it!"

"All right," puffed James. "You're on!"

"I'll show you who's fastest," chuffed Duncan. But Duncan was worried. James was big and strong. "I hope I can be as fast as James," he puffed nervously.

So Duncan delivered all his coal . . .
as fast as he could. "Must beat James! Must
beat James!" he puffed.

But when Duncan arrived back at the
wharf . . . James was waiting for him.

"I told you Main Line engines were the
fastest!" teased James.

Duncan looked at the long line of freight
cars. There was plenty of coal for the villages
there!

But Duncan didn't want to lose.

"Oh! Is this all you brought?" he tooted.
"The villages need lots more coal than that!"

"Then I'll bring more coal than you have
ever seen!" puffed James.

James raced back to the coaling plant.

And Duncan delivered the coal to the
villages.

Now all the villages had plenty of coal.

Duncan puffed back to the wharf.

But when Duncan arrived at the wharf, there were still lots more coal cars waiting. So Duncan decided to play a trick.

"I'll hide the coal cars before James gets back," he puffed.

Soon all the cars were hidden.

"Now James will think I've delivered all the coal," Duncan chuffed cheerfully.

James had collected lots more freight cars from the coaling plant. He was puffing harder than he had ever puffed before.

And he was using lots of coal.

At last, James arrived at the wharf.

There was Duncan!

"You still haven't brought enough coal!" teased Duncan. "I thought you were supposed to be Really Useful!"

"I'll soon be back with so much coal," puffed James, "it will take you all winter to deliver it!"

"Oh! We'll see!" puffed Duncan.

James still had to take the children to the concert. But he had been puffing so hard, he had used up all the coal in his tender! And soon . . . he ground to a halt!

That evening, the Narrow-Gauge Controller came to see Duncan.

"James is stuck. He has run out of coal," he announced. "Now he won't be able to take the children to the concert!"

Duncan felt terrible.

He thought about all the coal cars he had hidden. He thought about James, and then he thought about the children.

"I have to tell you about the hidden coal cars!" he *wheesh*ed.

The Narrow-Gauge Controller listened hard.

"You have caused delay and confusion," he said slowly. "But you have told the truth. And a Useful Engine always tells the truth."

"I'll only be a Really Useful Engine if I can help James," whistled Duncan.

So Duncan collected one of the coal cars he had hidden.

Snow started to fall.

Duncan rattled along the icy tracks.

Until, at last, Duncan found James.

"What are you doing here?" snorted James.

"I played a trick on you," chuffed Duncan. "I didn't take all the coal to the villages. I hid it from you!

"You are the fastest and a Really Useful Engine," Duncan added.

But James told Duncan that he was a Really Useful Engine, too.

"You brought the coal to me so quickly, I will still be able to take the children to the concert," he puffed. "Thank you, Duncan!"

The coal was quickly loaded into James' tender. Soon his fire was roaring and his boiler was as warm as toast.

He steamed off to collect the children.

Duncan felt happy.

"James is a Really Useful Engine!" puffed Duncan. "Ah! But then so am I!"

And he chuffed happily away to deliver more coal to the snowy villages.

• SEEING THE SIGHTS •

There are lots of wonderful sights to see on the Island of Sodor.
One summer's day, Thomas was given a very special job.

"Thomas," said Sir Topham Hatt, "you are to collect some very important visitors from the Mainland. They are arriving at Brendam Docks."

"Yes, Sir," tooted Thomas happily. "I will show them all the sights on Sodor!"

Thomas puffed happily towards Brendam Docks.

Thomas pulled up at the gangplank.

"Welcome aboard!" he tooted. "I will show you all the wonderful sights of Sodor!"

Just then, Gordon steamed in.

"I should be showing the sights to the important visitors," he sniffed.

"Why?" huffed Thomas.

"Because," *wheesh*ed Gordon, "I could show them round much more quickly than you. Then they would see everything there is to see on Sodor."

Thomas was cross. "I can show them all the sights just as quickly as you can!" he whistled. "Just you wait and see!"

Thomas heard passenger-car doors slam.

"Everyone's on board," he thought. And he chuffed away as quickly as he could. "So much to see, so much to see, let's get a move on, count on me."

Then there was trouble! Thomas had left some of the visitors behind!

Later, Thomas had to wait at a signal. Bertie the Bus drove up. He had picked up the visitors Thomas had left behind. Bertie honked his horn. But the signal had changed and Thomas puffed away. Thomas was in a hurry.

"Silly tank engine!" parped Bertie. "I will have to chase after you!"

The children on board Bertie thought a chase was great fun!

Thomas arrived at Black Loch. "Everyone out to see the seals," he tooted. "Hurry up, hurry up!"

The visitors took their cameras to see Black Loch.

Thomas had to wait. He didn't like waiting. He had to show the visitors all the sights.

"Otherwise," he thought, "I won't be as fast as Gordon."

"Time to go!" he peeped loudly.

Thomas heard a passenger-car door slam. "Everyone must be on board!" he thought. And Thomas chuffed away as fast as he could. But Thomas had left more of the visitors behind!

Soon Thomas arrived at the Scottish Castle.

"Everyone out," he peeped. "Hurry up, hurry up!"

Then Thomas had to wait again!

He *wheesh*ed some steam. And he started to worry.

"We'll never see everything if we don't hurry up!" Thomas *wheesh*ed. "Everyone back on board, please!"

Just then, Gordon steamed in. "Flatten my funnel!" sniffed Gordon. "You haven't seen many sights!"

"Yes, we have! And we're going to see more!" huffed Thomas. He *was* cross. He puffed away as quickly as he could . . . but more visitors were left behind.

Thomas steamed into the Fishing Village.

"Here's the next sight," he puffed. "Everybody out, please!" But Thomas couldn't hear any passenger-car doors opening. He was puzzled.

Just then, Bertie arrived.

"What's happening?" asked Thomas.

"No one's getting out, Thomas," beeped Bertie, "because no one is left on board!"

Thomas was surprised. "Cinders and ashes!" gasped Thomas.

"You were in so much of a hurry, you left them all behind."

Thomas was upset. "I must go back and pick everyone up!"

But first he collected the visitors from Bertie the Bus.

And he steamed back to the castle. He picked up his
passengers . . . and puffed quickly back to Black Loch.
  With all the visitors on board, Thomas set off again.

Thomas had to stop at a junction. He looked at the view of the sea. It was beautiful.

"I wish we could just stay here all day," Thomas *wheesh*ed. "There are so many things to do!"

The visitors looked out of the windows. Their faces smiled when they saw blue sea and the golden yellow sand.

Suddenly Thomas had an idea! "We *will* stay here all day," he whistled.

The visitors had a lovely time. Making sand castles . . . riding donkeys . . . and eating ice creams.

Thomas was very happy.

"You won't see all the sights eating ice creams," sniffed Gordon.

"It's better to see one place properly than lots of places in a hurry," Thomas chuffed happily.

And all the visitors agreed!